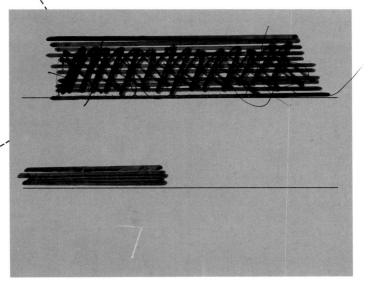

This book
belongs to

David&Charles
Children's Books

For Amelia with love M.N.

For Amy S.L.

First published in 1998 in Great Britain by Levinson Children's Books.
Published in this edition in 1999 by
David & Charles Children's Books,
Winchester House, 259-269 Old Marylebone Road,
London, NW1 5XJ

Text © Margaret Nash 1998
Illustrations © Stephen Lambert 1998

A CIP record for this title is available from the British Library.

The right of Margaret Nash and Stephen Lambert to be identified
as the author and illustrator of this work has been asserted by them
in accordance with the Copyright, Designs, and Patents Act, 1988.

ISBN 1-899607-98-6 hardback
ISBN 1-86233-057-3 paperback

Printed and bound in Belgium

SECRET in the MIST

Written by Margaret Nash

Illustrated by Stephen Lambert

David&Charles
Children's Books

Jonathan Quist had two secrets.

One was buried in a patch of sunny earth.

The other was buried in a patch of evening mist.

One morning Jonathan's mother opened the front door and saw something as thin as a pencil poking up from the patch of earth.

"What is that?" she asked.
"My secret," said Jonathan.
"My secret in the earth."

A secret in a patch of earth," she said. "How wonderful."

Jonathan's mother smiled and shook her duster so hard that golden dust specks slithered into the sunshine.

One evening as Daddy was
closing Jonathan's bedroom curtains,
he looked into a patch of purple mist
and saw something silver glimmering
in the moonshine.

"What's that?" asked Daddy.

"That's my secret," said Jonathan.

"My secret in the mist."

"A secret in the mist," said Daddy.

"That's really something, Jonathan."

He tucked Jonathan
into bed and went
downstairs.

The secret in the patch of sunny earth
grew as tall as the watering can and it had
two little leaves like ears.

The secret in the mist grew as tall as the cat's proud tail and it waved in the night air.

The secret in the patch of earth
grew as high as the door handle.

Jonathan clapped his hands.

"Keep going," cried Jonathan. It did.

The secret in the patch of evening mist
grew as high as the window-sill.

All the moths and fireflies danced around it,
and a spider spun a glinting cobweb above it.

Both secrets grew and grew.

One was nudged by sunshine

and laced with summer rain.

The other lived in silver shadows
and was stroked by bright white moonlight.

"Taller, taller," Jonathan told them both.

They grew taller and taller and taller!

The secret in the patch of earth reached up to Jonathan's bedroom and tapped against the window-pane.

His sister Kate opened the window.

"Whatever is that thing?" she asked Jonathan.

"Not telling," said Jonathan.

The secret in the evening mist swished against Jonathan's window and lulled him to sleep.

Next morning when Jonathan looked out of his bedroom window, he saw his mother standing on the lawn. And his father and his sister Kate.

He saw the postman standing by the gate,
and the delivery man walking by.
They were all staring up at something...

Jonathan pulled on his clothes and rushed downstairs.
Towering above everyone was an amazing flower.

It was larger than the clock's round face,

bolder than the blackbird's song
and more golden than the sunshine.

"That's the flashiest flower I've ever seen,"
said his sister Kate.

Everyone cheered. And next door's dog
barked for two whole minutes.

"That's the brightest secret I've ever seen," said his mother. "A giant sunflower. It's magnificent."

Jonathan smiled and thought about his secret in the mist.

That night Jonathan climbed out of bed and crept
downstairs. Daddy came out of the sitting room
to see what he wanted.

Together they stepped out into the garden.
Above them stood a mysterious shape like a silver crown.
It glistened in the moonlight. No one cheered
but Daddy hugged Jonathan,
and Jonathan hugged Teddy.

"That's the most beautiful secret I've ever seen,"
said Daddy. "A giant moonflower. It's magical."

The moon slid silently behind a cloud.

Then suddenly . . . just for a second, the flower's grey

stem turned green and the crown was tinged with gold.

"It's a sunflower by day
          and a moonflower by night,"
                              said Jonathan.

"So it is," said his parents. "How clever
of you to have made two secrets out of one!"

Other David & Charles Picture Books
for you to read:

Eggday
JOYCE DUNBAR • JANE CABRERA
hardback: 1 86233 100 6

Waiting For Baby
HARRIET ZIEFERT • EMILY BOLAM
hardback: 1 86233 125 1

Another Fine Mess
TONY BONNING • SALLY HOBSON
hardback: 1 86233 094 8
paperback: 1 86233 145 6

Hugo and the Bully Frogs
FRANCESCA SIMON • CAROLINE JAYNE CHURCH
hardback: 1 86233 093 X

Animal ABC
DAVID WOJTOWYCZ
hardback: 1 86233 107 3

David&Charles
Children's Books